Pebble® Plus
Bilingüe/Bilingual

Exploremos la galaxia/Exploring the Galaxy
La Luna/The Moon

por/by Thomas K. Adamson

Traducción/Translation: Dr. Martín Luis Guzmán Ferrer

Editor Consultor/Consulting Editor: Dra. Gail Saunders-Smith

Consultor/Consultant: Dr. Roger D. Launius
Chair, Division of Space History
National Air and Space Museum
Smithsonian Institution, Washington, D.C.

Capstone
press®

Mankato, Minnesota

Pebble Plus is published by Capstone Press,
151 Good Counsel Drive, P.O. Box 669, Mankato, Minnesota 56002.
www.capstonepress.com

1 2 3 4 5 6 13 12 11 10 09 08

Library of Congress Cataloging-in-Publication Data
Adamson, Thomas K., 1970–
    [Moon. Spanish & English]
    La Luna / por Thomas K. Adamson = The moon / by Thomas K. Adamson.
    p. cm. — (Pebble plus. Exploremos la galaxia = Exploring the galaxy)
    Includes index.
    ISBN-13: 978-1-4296-0047-7 (hardcover)
    ISBN-10: 1-4296-0047-0 (hardcover)
    1. Moon — Juvenile literature. I. Title. II. Series.
QB582.A3318 2008
523.3 — dc22   2007003489

Summary: Simple text and photographs describe Earth's moon — in both English and Spanish.

Editorial Credits
Katy Kudela, bilingual editor; Eida del Risco, Spanish copy editor; Kia Adams, set designer; Mary Bode,
    book designer and illustrator; Jo Miller, photo researcher/photo editor

Photo Credits
Astronomical Society of the Pacific, 19
Getty Images Inc./The Image Bank/Theo Allofs, 7; Stone/Ron Dahlquist, 10–11
Grant Heilman Photography/Chad Ehlers, 4–5
NASA, 21
Photodisc, 9 (both), 13 (both)
Photo Researchers, Inc./NASA, 15, 17
Shutterstock/Carolina K. Smith, M.D., 1; David Woods, cover

Note to Parents and Teachers

The Exploremos la galaxia/Exploring the Galaxy set supports national science standards related to earth
science. This book describes and illustrates la Luna/the Moon in both English and Spanish. The photographs
support early readers in understanding the text. The repetition of words and phrases helps early readers learn
new words. This book also introduces early readers to subject-specific vocabulary words, which are defined in
the Glossary section. Early readers may need assistance to read some words and to use the Table of Contents,
Glossary, Internet Sites, and Index sections of the book.

Table of Contents

Tabla de contenidos

The Moon

The Moon is the brightest
object in the night sky.
It reflects the Sun's light.

La Luna

La Luna es el objeto que más
brilla en el cielo por la noche.
La Luna refleja la luz del Sol.

The Moon seems to change
shape during the month.
The Moon can look round
like a circle. It can look
narrow like a banana.

La Luna parece cambiar
de forma durante el mes.
Puede verse redonda como
un círculo. Puede verse tan
delgada como un plátano.

The Moon and Earth

The Moon is Earth's satellite.
It moves around Earth once
each month. The same side
of the Moon always faces Earth.

La Luna y la Tierra

La Luna es el satélite de la Tierra.
Da una vuelta alrededor de
la Tierra una vez al mes.
El mismo lado de la Luna
siempre mira hacia la Tierra.

Earth/Tierra

Moon/Luna

The Moon shines brightly
at night. It looks lighter
in the day.

La Luna brilla intensamente
durante la noche. Por el
día se ve más clara.

The Moon is much smaller
than Earth. If Earth were a
tennis ball, the Moon would
be the size of a marble.

La Luna es mucho más pequeña
que la Tierra. Si la Tierra fuera
una pelota de tenis, la Luna
sería del tamaño de una canica.

Earth/
Tierra

Moon/
Luna

The Moon's Surface

Gray dust and rocks

cover the Moon.

The Moon's surface

is rough.

La superficie de la Luna

La Luna está cubierta

de polvo gris y rocas.

La superficie de la Luna

es rugosa.

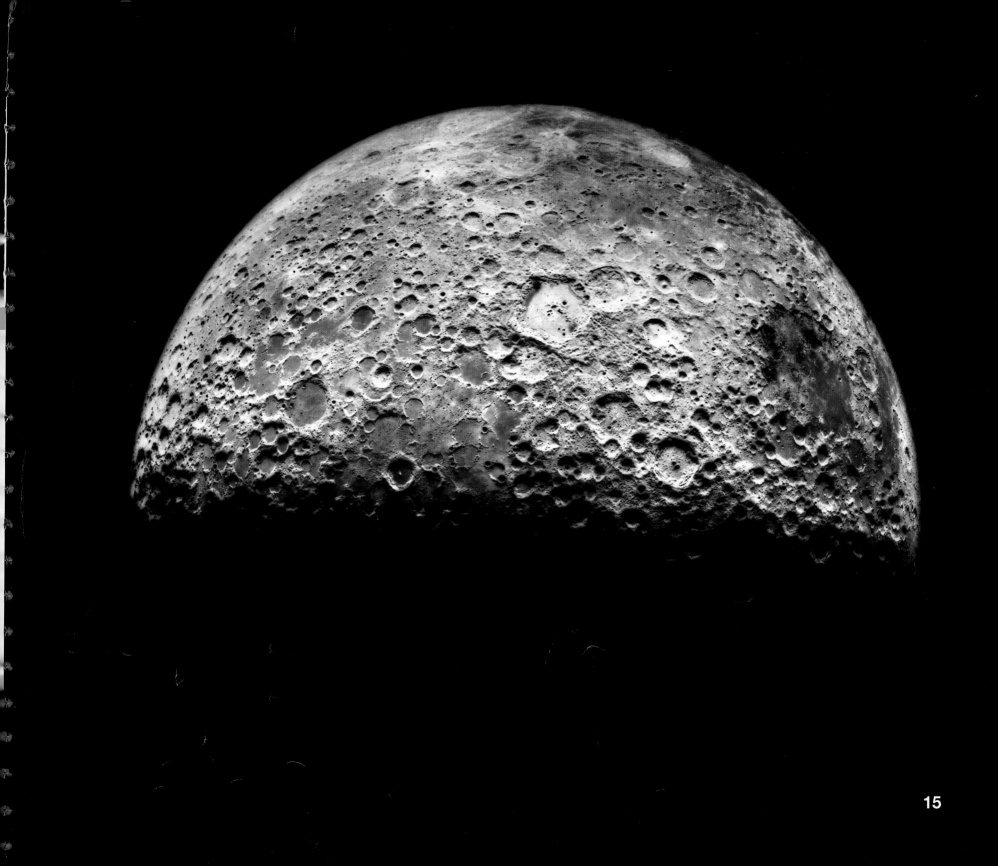

Craters make the Moon's surface
bumpy. These holes formed
when objects hit the Moon.

Los cráteres hacen que la superficie
de la Luna esté llena de baches.
Estos agujeros se formaron por el
impacto de objetos contra la Luna.

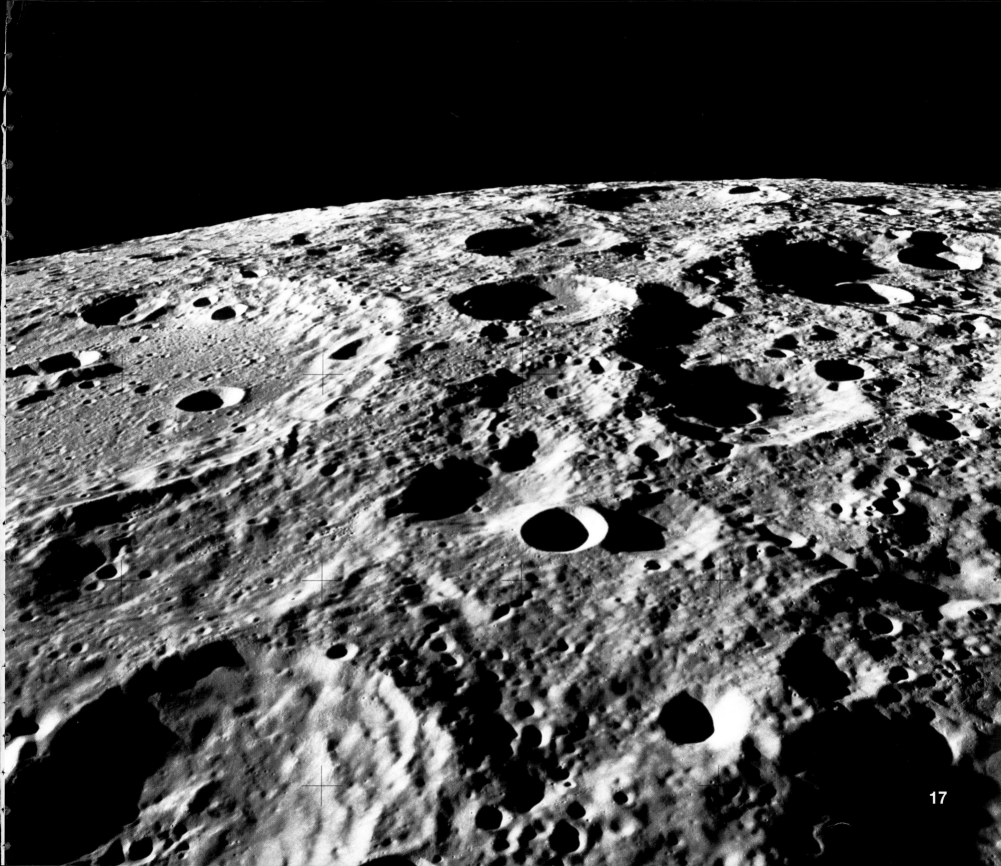

The Moon is not like Earth.

The Moon has no air or water.

The sky is always black.

La Luna no es como la Tierra.

La Luna no tiene aire ni agua.

Su cielo siempre está negro.

Exploring the Moon

Astronauts have landed on
the Moon six times.
They gathered rocks
and soil to study.

Explorando la Luna

Los astronautas han llegado
seis veces a la Luna.
Ellos recogieron rocas y
tierra para estudiarlas.

Glossary

astronaut — a person who travels into space

crater — a hole made when objects crash into a planet's or moon's surface

Earth — the planet we live on

reflect — to return light from an object; the Moon reflects light from the Sun.

satellite — an object that travels around another object in space; the Moon is Earth's satellite.

Sun — the star that Earth and the other planets move around; the Sun provides light and heat for the planets.

surface — the outside or outermost area of something

Glosario

el astronauta — persona que viaja al espacio

el cráter — agujero formado por el impacto de objetos contra la superficie de un planeta o una luna

reflejar — cuando un objeto devuelve la luz que recibe; la Luna refleja la luz del Sol.

el satélite — objeto que se mueve alrededor de otro objeto en el espacio

el Sol — estrella alrededor de la que giran la Tierra y los otros planetas; el Sol proporciona luz y calor a los planetas.

la superficie — la parte de afuera o más externa de algo

la Tierra — el planeta en el que vivimos

Internet Sites

FactHound offers a safe, fun way to find Internet sites related to this book. All of the sites on FactHound have been researched by our staff.

Here's how:

1. Visit *www.facthound.com*

2. Choose your grade level.

3. Type in this book ID **1429600470** for age-appropriate sites. You may also browse subjects by clicking on letters, or by clicking on pictures and words.

4. Click on the **Fetch It** button.

FactHound will fetch the best sites for you!

Index

Sitios de Internet

FactHound te brinda una manera divertida y segura de encontrar sitios de Internet relacionados con este libro. Hemos investigado todos los sitios de FactHound. Es posible que algunos sitios no estén en español.

Se hace así:

1. Visita *www.facthound.com*

2. Elige tu grado escolar.

3. Introduce este código especial **1429600470** para ver sitios apropiados a tu edad, o usa una palabra relacionada con este libro para hacer una búsqueda general.

4. Haz un clic en el botón **Fetch It**.

¡FactHound buscará los mejores sitios para ti!

Índice